# PADDINGTON™

HarperFestival is an imprint of HarperCollins Publishers.

Paddington: Paddington's World
Based on the Paddington novels written and created by Michael Bond
PADDINGTON™ and PADDINGTON BEAR™ © Paddington and Company Limited/
STUDIOCANAL S.A. 2014
www.harpercollinschildrens.com
ISBN 978-0-06-234997-2
14 15 16 17 18   LP   10 9 8 7 6 5 4 3 2
❖
First Edition

# PADDINGTON™

## Paddington's World

Adapted by Annie Auerbach and Mandy Archer

Based on the screenplay written by Paul King

Based on the Paddington Bear novels

written and created by Michael Bond

HARPER FESTIVAL

*An Imprint of HarperCollinsPublishers*

Paddington Bear arrived in London after a
long journey at sea. He'd stowed away on a ship.

Paddington can't wait to see London—he wants to visit Buckingham Palace, travel on the Underground, and finally meet Big Ben! But first, the Brown family is going to take him back to 32 Windsor Gardens.

Taxi

Oh, dear. The taxi driver has gotten in a muddle with his directions. Choose the right route to the Browns' house.

A    B

NATURAL HISTORY MUSEUM

WINDSOR GARDENS

Trafalgar Square

Lambeth Bridge

Paddington was looking for a new home. He tried to ask for help, but many people passed by him without noticing the small bear.

Luckily, the Browns stopped to help. They offered him a place to stay for the night. Mrs. Brown even gave Paddington his name.

The following day, Mrs. Brown took Paddington to meet an old friend of hers. His name was Mr. Gruber.

"He knows all about lost worlds and hidden treasures," she said.

Paddington hoped that Mr. Gruber would help him find the old explorer who had visited his aunt and uncle in Peru.

While they were visiting Mr. Gruber, Paddington spotted a thief. He raced out of the shop door and chased the thief through the city. Mr. Gruber was thrilled that Paddington had been able to help.

# Lost in London

**START**

Poor Paddington is somewhere in the capital city—lost, lonely, and almost certainly in trouble! Can you help the Brown family track down the young bear? Weave a route through the London landmarks, avoiding the dead ends and blind alleys.

FINISH

While Paddington was finding his way around London and searching for the explorer, someone else was searching for him. The director of taxidermy at the Natural History Museum was determined to find a rare animal to add to her large collection. Her name was Millicent.

# Paddington's Scrapbook

Paddington has gathered some of his favorite photographs together and put them in an album. Whenever he feels sad or lonely, the bear can go up to the Browns' attic and cheer himself up again!

Paddington needs to write some captions for these pages, but Mrs. Bird has called him down for tea. Could you finish the job for him? Write an imaginative description underneath each shot.

The Brown family was very welcoming when I arrived in London.

..........................................

..........................................

..........................................

..........................................

..........................................

..........................................

....................................

....................................

....................................

## Super scrapbooking

Starting a scrapbook is easy—all you need is an album or journal—even a lined notebook will do! Here are Paddington's tips for recording your own magical memories.

1. Stick, stick, stick!
   A scrapbook doesn't have to be limited to photos. Postcards, ticket stubs, stickers, and leaflets will all make your pages interesting to read and look back on.

2. Decorate the pages.
   Use ink stamps, felt pens, and crayons to fill up any spare space with notes, cartoons, and pictures. It's a chance to really get creative!

3. Save the date!
   Whenever you can remember the date of an event or special occasion, write it in your scrapbook. When you look back in the future, it will help you place how old you were when it happened.

Paddington was beginning to adjust to life with the Browns.
He had many things to learn about living in England, though.

Paddington missed Peru and his aunt Lucy, who had stayed behind at the Home for Retired Bears in Lima. He wrote her postcards, but he wished she could be with him to see all the sights and sounds of London for herself.

# Puzzling Peru

When he's not taking his chances on the busy streets of London, Paddington often stops to think about Darkest Peru. It was a place where he could sit in his tree house and eat marmalade all day long.

## RAIN FOREST

The lush, natural ecosystem that covers nearly two-thirds of Paddington's homeland.

## ANDES

The majestic mountain range that runs through this South American country.

## LAKE TITICACA

The world's highest navigable lake. It can be found in Southern Peru.

## LIMA

The capital of Peru and home to over a quarter of the population.

## NUEVO SOL

The currency of Peru.

## CERRO BLANCO

The highest sand dune on the planet is Peruvian. It towers over the Sechura Desert.

## FIESTAS PATRIAS

Every July, Peru celebrates its independence from the Spanish. The official celebrations last three days.

## ORCHID

Peru's climate is perfect for growing orchids. It can boast 1,500 different types of this flower.

## GUINEA PIG

Peruvians call these *cuy.*

## GOLD

Peru is rich in natural resources. As well as gold, its lands are mined for silver, copper, lead, and zinc.

## MACHU PICCHU

An ancient Incan mountaintop citadel that can be visited to this day.

## BIRDS

Peru has the most bird species in the entire world. There are also huge numbers of butterflies.

## AMAZON

The world's largest tropical rain forest. Only Brazil has more Amazon jungle than Peru.

## POTATO

Wild potatoes first originated from Peru. There are now at least a thousand different types.

## QUECHUA

One of Peru's official languages. The others are Spanish and Aymara.

Read all about the Peruvian words and phrases, then look for them in the word search below!

```
W  D  K  Q  U  E  C  H  U  A  H  P  T  I  L
R  R  X  B  A  J  C  L  O  S  O  V  E  U  N
A  Y  K  D  M  T  T  D  T  S  I  Q  H  E  H
I  O  C  N  A  L  B  O  R  R  E  C  O  F  S
N  D  P  T  Z  M  N  X  S  N  C  R  X  F  B
F  L  A  G  O  U  G  K  L  I  C  K  R  N  J
O  B  I  J  N  H  P  K  P  H  D  P  G  C  C
R  F  C  M  S  M  G  U  I  N  E  A  P  I  G
E  N  S  H  A  R  H  D  Y  O  O  A  S  M  O
S  D  E  V  E  C  S  S  I  L  T  L  E  W  L
T  O  D  M  A  W  D  A  T  O  W  A  X  M  D
Y  E  N  M  H  X  R  U  V  Y  O  V  T  U  S
A  C  A  C  I  T  I  T  E  K  A  L  G  O  Z
Z  L  Q  Q  J  K  B  F  U  Q  Z  R  Y  B  P
R  F  I  E  S  T  A  S  P  A  T  R  I  A  S
```

Paddington thought he had overstayed his welcome at the Browns' house. He packed his suitcase and went in search of the explorer. He met Millicent, who told him that she could help him. Paddington was so eager to find a home that he went with Millicent to the museum.

But when the Browns discovered Paddington was gone, they went searching for him. They had come to love Paddington. At the museum, the entire family worked together to stop Millicent from hurting Paddington.

Then Paddington went back to Number 32
Windsor Gardens with the Browns. He had
found the home he'd been searching for all along.

# Postcards to Peru

Paddington is a loyal nephew—he always remembers to write to his aunt Lucy back at the Home for Retired Bears in Peru. Look at his latest batch of postcards. Can you work out where Paddington has been visiting?

Read each postcard, then match it to the correct London landmark.

**1.**
Dear Aunt Lucy,

Today Judy and Jonathan took me on an enormous Ferris wheel. Instead of carriages, we rode in giant glass pods. What breathtaking views!

Paddington x

**3.**
To my adoring aunt,

I met my delightful new friend Mr. Gruber this morning. We visited an old building with an impressive domed roof. Did you know it was designed by Sir Christopher Wren?

Paddington x

**2.**
Hello from London!

The city does have such a lot of history! Today I went to its very center. I paddled in fountains and saluted Admiral Nelson. He was standing at the top of his very own column!

Paddington x

**4.**
Dear Aunt Lucy,

This evening Mrs. Brown decided that it was time for some culture! We watched a Shakespeare play in an open-air venue on the banks of the River Thames. Bravo!

Paddington x

A. The Globe Theatre postcard ☐

C. The London Eye postcard ☐

B. St. Paul's Cathedral postcard ☐

D. Trafalgar Square postcard ☐

Answers: A=4, B=3, C=1, D=2